Highway B: Horrorfest

Brantly Martin

Published in the United States by:
Archway Editions,
a division of powerHouse Cultural Entertainment, Inc.
32 Adams Street, Brooklyn, NY 11201

www.archwayeditions.us

Daniel Power, CEO
Chris Molnar, Editorial Director
Nicodemus Nicoludis, Managing Editor
Naomi Falk, Editor

Library of Congress Control Number: 2022940727

ISBN 978-1-64823-010-3

Printed by Toppan Leefung

First edition, 2023

10 9 8 7 6 5 4 3 2 1

Edited by Naomi Falk
Design by Robert Avellan with Chris Molnar

Printed and bound in China

ARCHWAY
EDITIONS

Highway B: Horrorfest

Brantly Martin

Archway Editions, Brooklyn, NY

CONTENTS

l'ALBERGO SPIRITUS

In a fishing village across the bay from l'Albergo Spiritus all residents are required to write a story upon waking. This must be done every day and the story must be titled l'Albergo Spiritus. The town elders then gather and read through the stories and choose which l'Albergo Spiritus is to be the basis of reality that day. Once per year, on No Story Day, the requirement is lifted and all hell breaks loose and all are reminded of the reason realities are based on stories.

The town elders rejected that story and reject all stories suggesting a No Story Day.

The following story was not rejected:

l'Albergo Spiritus

It's rumored that l'Albergo Spiritus has one room and one bed and one candle and one view and one book of prayers. Stays are for one extinction only and guests arrive by way of fishing boat. It's said by some that the inn is the oldest on B and it's said by some that the inn is not of B and it's said by some that the inn was long ago washed away and it's said by former guests of l'Albergo

Spiritus that the fishing village across the bay is a simulation gulag that mines stories and sells them to the simulation resort l'Albergo Spiritus.

VEEL

A jilted lover placed a curse on Veel. Only the jilted lover had not been jilted by Veel, she had been jilted by Zeel. Somewhere inside the frequency upon which one doles out curses, Veel had been mistaken for Zeel. How often this happens on B—a curse landing off course—has never been determined. Some theorists put it at fifty percent, others higher still. If this is true, then to live in a land whose inhabitants, at least once in their life, cast a curse, is to live in a land where at least half the inhabitants have been unjustly cursed. Of course, those unjustly cursed would have likely been cursed anyway, perhaps with a far more malevolent curse. And then there are those deserving of curses who manage to live and die curse-free.

BESTIARY: THE LODOFLOR

*The Lodoflor was a bird of burden destined to
carry wayward ideas.*

Ideas on B were once autonomous, free to do as they pleased. Often, these ideas found their creators repugnant. Often, these ideas rejected the idea that their creators had created them. Often, these ideas had ideas of their own and those ideas became the burden of the Lodoflor. This burden proved fatal: the Lodoflor no longer soared, no longer flew, lost its wings and buried itself and its burden of wayward ideas in subterranean citadels accessible only to the underworld.

*The Lodoflor is often mistaken for the Movoflor, the bird of prey
destined to retrieve ideas from the underworld.*

DEATH RATTLE OF A SPECIES

LaNota, a character in a horror simulation, made a name for herself recording death rattles. Her first death rattle recording was an accident: as an infant she levitated out of her crib and began speaking in tongues; her mother died of shock but not before letting rip with a death rattle captured by the simulation's security system that LaNota integrated years later into her first album, *Death Rattles Tattle Tattle*.

Every creature on B has a unique death rattle and LaNota was not the first to record them but was the first to postulate that within these collective death rattles was a musicality, a secret language that held all the answers to the universe (or at least to her simulation).

•

After releasing her sixteenth album of death rattle operas, LaNota—now The Death Rattle Queen and famous within certain avant-garde circles—set her sights on something grander: the death rattle of a species.

•

LaNota gave clever interviews and wrote elegant essays on the profundity of what she'd discovered recording *Death Rattle of a Species*. Photo shoots were arranged and cover art was circulated and concert dates were set and all was in its proper place . . . unfortunately there *was* no recording, as no species on B (or its simulations) was under threat of extinction.

LaNota set out to find the most isolated species on B and discovered a species of serpentine elves called Nae that lived at the bottom of a lake near B's southern pole. LaNota set up underwater recording devices, poisoned the lake, and recorded the death rattle of the Nae.

•

Death Rattle of a Species thrust LaNota into the mainstream and anointed her The Conservation Queen, after the extinction of the Nae created a chain reaction of other species going extinct, each one getting its own album of death rattles.

SEX PARTY: SKETCH ORGIES

By decree, the city of Prabang was now the city of Abstainia and the citizens of Abstainia, formerly the citizens of Prabang, were no longer permitted to engage in sex parties. In fact, the citizens of Abstainia were no longer permitted to engage in fornication or masturbation of any persuasion. They were monitored by nanobots floating throughout their bodies that they had volunteered, under much different auspices, to have introduced. Any deviations into past deviancy would result in "death by nanobot": pain pain painful. All births in Abstainia were to be celebrations of DNA breakthroughs and cloning conquests. Unbeknownst to the "liberators of Prabang"—the new rulers of Abstainia, a clan of mutated zealots—the only sex Prabangians engaged in was sex party sex. In response, and with grand hopes of a coming revolution, the Abstainians née Prabangians began to gather for weekly Sketch Orgies. Each sex party attendee arrived with a sketch pad, stripped naked, and sketched the most lewd, debaucherous, sometimes sensual and often scandalous, sex operas one could imagine if one was sketching naked and denied sex. The more gifted of the Abstainian artists went on to oil paintings, frescoes, sculptures, even orgy-adorned sarcophagi. Centuries later, when these artifacts were recovered after the Orgasmic War, the Cult of Abstainia became synonymous, not without irony, with sexual freedom.

THE PUB OF THE PEEK A'LOWS

There is a pub in the former immigrant former gay former artist former inexpensive quarter of the city that was formerly the epicenter of B's foremost literary movement. The movement never had a former name—they never got around to it—but is now most commonly referred to as Speculative Procrastination. The movement consisted of various writers, thinkers, philosophers, and conjurers gathering daily at The Pub of the Peek a'Lows (a rather tiny pub) and, armed with nothing more than silence and a pint, envisioning all the novels, treatises, poems, and essays they would one day write. To be clear: they didn't envision fame or riches, or even respect and admiration: they envisioned all of the words and all of the punctuation and all of the fonts and all of the spacing and all of the art and all of the binding and all of the details to all of their books down to the source of the paper.

One day a Speculative Procrastinationist blurted out that she was to begin writing: she went to the nearest stationary store, bought supplies, returned to the pub, and began. The rest of the movement followed suit—except for l'Uno.

The literary movement that followed was called One Go because all of the books were written in one go, having already been envisioned and memorized by their authors. Slowly the One Goers became minor or major celebrities or intellectuals and lost all interest in writing except when they were being paid to write about their former writing. They scattered to all the major cities of B as their former quarter was gentrified, stripped of all eccentricities and oddities, and reimagined as a progressive, efficient and modern "hub of ideas." The owner of The Pub of the Peek a'Lows, however, refused to sell as long as l'Uno refused to begin writing. And refuse he did. The new residents of the quarter found The Pub of the Peek a'Lows "charming" and "quaint" but found the presence of l'Uno—sipping a pint and staring blankly into the world of the unwritten—rather disturbing and incongruous. When the owner of the pub died, his daughter, the new owner, built a wall around l'Uno that became The l'Uno Room. The residents were pleased and l'Uno was indifferent: he carried on sipping and staring. It's unknown if he ever wrote a book.

TIME-RELEASE NARCISSISM IN A PILL

A woman forgotten to history invented a pill that time-released narcissism. The woman for whom this woman worked was a woman of great means and greater intelligence: all those who studied with her, sparred with her, fornicated with her, or worked for her called her La'Ma and she would go on to bring the world a technological utopia that opened frontiers, saved lives, fostered peace, and rightfully and righteously anointed her the only genius of her era. (An era upended four generations later by, depending on one's perspective, a "band of well-armed puritanical luddites," or "freedom fighters for neurological autonomy.")

La'Ma's greatest gift, however, was deducing the lay of the land and her place in it.

•

The social scorecards and dopamine cocktails that governed the interface into the (back then) only accessible timeline gave an outsized advantage to those blessed to be pure and proper narcissists. La'Ma surmised that this was not only true now, but would continue to be true for the duration of her change-the-world window. La'Ma also knew she'd been born without this blessing, had never acquired it, and would never be able to talk about and transmit about and hero's-journey about herself in kaleidoscoping perpetuity.

"Narcissism," concluded La'Ma, "is my generation's only gatekeeper."

And so, under strict confidence, she hired the soon-to-be disappeared woman to run a department of one, with the sole purpose of mining, refining, and replicating the neurological pathways of the world's foremost narcissists. Her mission was to create a pill that would allow La'Ma to put herself at the center of the story, talk not about her ideas or her mission but about *La'Ma La'Ma La'Ma* as an indispensable force—an iconoclast!—whenever and wherever and for however long was needed. (And without a trace of humility.)

The pill was perfected and La'Ma promised herself that as soon as her mission to better the world was on its irreversible path she'd share her story and share her pill with those suffering from the same lack of narcissism in a world designed for narcissists.

The pill—or, more precisely, the intermittent states of fully-realized narcissism that La'Ma began to more frequently ("for the good of all") self-induce—proved as transformative as La'Ma's vision of a better world. La'Ma's profile was raised and her company soared and all of B sped toward a more amicable and civilized state.

•

La'Ma began to double dose . . . triple dose . . . binge . . .

These binges, La'Ma was certain, were the very reason for a better world which meant *she* was the reason for a better world and any "leveling of the playing field" she had formerly considered would do just the opposite as she was the only one capable of leveraging narcissism without falling victim to it: *she couldn't allow knowledge of the pill to get out* . . .

•

The woman that invented the pill that time-released narcissism was sent on a company-sponsored satellite retreat from which she never returned.

After solving much of B's ills, La'Ma spent the last quarter of her life creating a subscription-based lifestyle brand named La'Ma that promised to reshape its users in her likeness. Her posthumous memoir, *La Da D La La'Ma*, remained atop the best seller list until all books were recommissioned as time-release pills.

BESTIARY: THE SNITH

Sniths were once The Sniths, a noble family of disorienting wealth and hermetic taste.

The Sniths hailed from a mountainous region of B immune to passage and long engulfed in low-hanging folklore. This noble family's unwavering isolation and aversion to Culture—their devout Absence—opened the very space, created the very channel, from which the masses below whispered a caricatured and blasphemous version of The Sniths into existence.

This violation turned The Sniths further inward and into the arms of scientific innovation and devout incest.

There has been much debate and lunar dust-fueled speculation on whether it was the science or the incest that transformed noble to beast. There has also been speculation, often whispered, that perhaps noble has transformed to *nobler*. (More radical whispers challenge the very notion of *bestiary* as a legitimate taxonomy.)

The Sniths pursued their science and hid their penchant for

incestual relations for centuries . . . lunar dusts were drained of knowledge . . . incestual offspring were examined to death, sacrificed to the gods of self-propulsion and time-bent determinism . . . scientific progress was trial-and-error forged until, finally, a compromise with immortality was reached and one member of The Sniths looked precisely like all other members of The Sniths.

And they looked as one would imagine an inconvenient perfection to look.

Regarding the morality below . . .

Much was whispered and much was left unspoken and more was forgotten. Ultimately, morality itself was frozen inside a perverse détente between Isolation and Culture.

The Snith joined the bestiary.

JINGLE JAMES

Jingle James is a crooner, performance poet, anti-realist, latent spiritualist, sometimes thespian, angular ventriloquist, custom hat collector, psalm enabler, resigned collagist, three-piece-suit hole-burner, and intermittent recluse. For some, he's the interdimensional bridge from forgotten to speculative. For others, he's an autoconstructed fraud, a pernicious huckster.

Jingle James has many personae: Gin Jim, Sin Jim, Binge Jim, and Blame James to name a few. More than anything else, Jingle James is known for what's called Jimmy's Jingles. These jingles are an admixture of rant, ballad, advert for the abyss, vomit, autoimmune corrective, lunar dust hypnagogic, and cultural x-ray. He's performed thousands of jingles and written even more. His jingles tend to begin within one cirrus vibration then shift to another then another. He's never talked about the derivation or destination of these jingles—nor, for that matter, has he spoken of anything. Jingle James exists between diverging natures of reality. In the first, one might overhear: I'd love to fuck Jingle James; in the other, one might declare: *Jingle James & Jimmy Jingles / Oh to fuck a single jingle.*

HOKA

Origins of a genocidal meme.

Hoka grew up on a hard drive for abandoned dreams. Whether or not Hoka remained a dream during his time on the hard drive is a philosophical question that begs more philosophical questions, such as: Is a dream abandoned still a dream? And: Does a recovered dream differ from a recurring dream? Hoka's time on the hard drive was marked by the twin abuses of muted recollection and corporeal dissonance. Hoka promised himself that, one day, once recurring, his body of work would never fade.

Hoka began as an idea: a shared idea between two divergent idealists. The first idealist never lacked for ideas: ideas flowed through her like solar flares through a satellite villa. The second idealist was forever starved for ideas: ideas treated him like autonomy treats a marionette. This mismatched couple proved tragic in their assessment of ideas: the first ever ambivalent, the second ever keen. This produced Hoka: an inevitable and fleeting idea for those who flow with ideas, and a doomed and cataclysmic seduction for those who construct the ideas of others.

SIMULATION VERSUS LUNAR DUST

A simulation named *Ca'bal* (a simulation loosely based on the classic children's fable *A Cannibal of One's Own*) is released prior to each extinction event on B.

Ca'bal begins with the simulatee dining at a no-frills establishment also named Ca'bal. The simulatee is meant to eat—carve up and, if one so chooses, broil, fry, or sear—a version of themselves that is dutifully laid out on a marble slab functioning as a spartan dining table. The would-be meal is the simulatee's better, perhaps best, self. A dream version. All who simulate inside *Ca'bal* are promised healing, knowledge, acceptance: promised a fresh—if bloody and snake-oily—slate. All the simulatee contributes is an appetite.

That isn't true of course, but that's invariably how the effects of the lunar dust Ca'bal come on: that's the dimension it opens up and expounds from: that's the key in which it sings.

The lunar dust Ca'bal has never been "discovered," it no longer exists on B's moons and is believed to reside, in altered form, in the guts of a rarely-seen tribe partial to the brackish waters of B's lower gulf coast. This tribe is rumored to be asexual, spritely non-secular, and something of an agreed upon illusion awaiting its archetypal etching . . . and yet this tribe has survived all of B's extinction events.

This tribe is also rumored to sacrifice its elders via cannibalism before purging their remains into those brackish waters and releasing Ca'bal into the ecosystem, beginning a cycle of narcissism, decadence, amnesia, and extinction—beginning the cycle of illusory battles described in the epic poem *A Cannibal of One's Own*.

That's not true either, other than the part about *dimension* and *key*. The true nature and source of the lunar dust Ca'bal will be revealed right here, in the operatic simulation *A Cannibal of One's Own*, and the only regard in which this simulation differs from the simulation *Ca'bal* is that here the simulatee is the meal, and here the simulatee is the lunar dust Ca'bal and here the extinction event is always underway.

All of that is true enough, but this is truer:

The lunar dust Ca'bal resides in the guts of every sentient being on B. It settled there long ago when B's hierophants became lunar dusts and B's archetypes were commodified as simulations.

THE ORGANMEISTER

An anonymous prankster and cheeky inventor brought B—or at least the social slices of B that appreciate pranks and cheekiness—the organmeister. Part church organ and part cellular tickler, the organmeister has become the center of a pranky and cheeky cult that can be found gathering in abandoned churches for Organmeister Fests. It goes like this . . .

The church organ is tuned and calibrated to something called the *quantum organmeister frequency* in a ceremony performed by one of four roving organmeister meisters. After this is done, every major organ of the body is at the mercy of the church organ and an orgy of suffering and ecstasy, orgasms and bowel movements, appendicitises and liver failures, gall bladder bounces and kidney regenerations ensue. The kids can't get enough.

The four roving organmeister meisters have sworn an oath to carry the secrets of the organmeister to the graves they intend to send themselves to, in due time, via the organmeister.

THE SENTENCING OF NANT & NIGN

Nant and Nign never spent a day apart. They traveled, separately, to the far ends of B. They deep dived, separately, inside lunar dust tales. They made love, fornicated—fuck fuck fucked—simultaneously in satellite villas above opposing hemispheres. But they never spent a day apart.

They'd been assigned to the same Dub Life subscription, an error on the part of Dub Life, and one—after the subsequent exposure—that ultimately sank Dub Life. A sinking that led to the underground (and now affordable) trend of syncing lives: YOU ARE BUT ONE EYE IN GEMINI read the ubiquitous holographic murals of an intertwined Nant and Nign.

Nant and Nign became the reluctant faces of an underground, of a *cool*, that shunned any and all who chose not to sync their life with another, and often *others*.

A fog of codependence moved in, a charming dictator in its wake. This dictator—an heiress—declared that all must sync lives with her and her alone. She sentenced Nant and Nign, now the somewhat *less* reluctant faces of the underground, to a public separation, sentenced them as a warning to all who would sync lives with anyone but her.

It worked . . .

Nant and Nign, unable to experience life alone, committed suicide (well, the closest thing to suicide algorithmic hallucinations can commit) soon after and the underground syncing of lives gave way to a rather humdrum religion.

However . . .

A sexual revolution spread across B, one that reimagined the motivation of future dictators.

NÖS & SÖN

The twin islands of Nös and Sön have a perverse symbiosis. Once a single island, they were separated by a volcanic eruption or an earthquake or a tsunami or, if you believe in latent mythologies and vengeful coding, separated by experimental geosadism. At the time of their separation they were uninhabited and none of their future inhabitants would ever know of their separation trauma.

They longed for each other like incestuous lovers.

Nös became the island of elevated taste, of refined aesthetics. This left Nös open to various totalitarian movements but shielded it from the depravity of consumer and corporate decadence: a decadence most often manifested in sameness and regression to a manufactured mean. Sön became the island of punishment, of re-education and reformation. The philosophy behind Sön's internment program, its hands-free torture, was the celebration of mediocrity. As Nös refined and elevated its architecture, language, dress, song, dance, art . . . Sön refined its mediocrity. A point was reached where one raised on Nös could bear no more than a few days on Sön without breaking: a point was reached where mediocrity-immersion functioned as an incision-free lobotomy for those that had never been exposed to even trace amounts of mediocrity.

RED LIGHT DISTRICT OF KLADOW

Unlike most red light districts, the red light district of Kladow still trades in flesh. Its customers provide the flesh and it goes like this . . .

Anyone, for a fee, can provide their DNA and authorize a clone to be made of their "sex self." Of the version of themselves they've been trained to exploit yet never explore. It takes about a week for this clone to fully form—to be "dimmed lights ready." Once ready this clone is for hire in whatever role its Original approves: dominant or submissive or anything in-between. Originals often attend their clone's sessions, observing their sex self behind the artificial intelligence of a one-way mirror.

LUNAR DUST DREAMS

I dreamed I was alone on a satellite villa . . . before going to bed, in the dream, I set the filtration system to CALM . . . when I woke, in the dream, it was set to CHAOS . . . I dreamed this was no longer my dream . . . someone else was dreaming Highway B and in the dream I knew who she was.

I dreamed I was the owner of a lunar dust bar that served only one lunar dust, which was, in the dream, the only lunar dust I did not abstain from. I was also a patron at the bar. The bar, long ago, was called Highway B and had undergone many iterations and many appellations and was once again, under the new ownership, called Highway B. The patron version of myself held court at the center of a black banquette inside a mural of a mirror. When the effects of the lunar dust subsided, the patron holding court was no longer a version of myself, but was a disjointed blue-tinted avian cherub.

I dreamed I wasn't myself, I wasn't B: I was "B." I'm sure you know what I mean. I was B in the voice of escapism . . . escapism painted in a surreal and stoned clock hue of . . . escapism . . .

Time in this dream was LESS BUT BETTER.

Colors in this dream were MORE BUT INSECURE.

Geometry in this dream was untrustworthy and all communication with other—dare I say—*beings* in this dream was nonverbal, melodic and violent and free of miserly virtues and hypnotic contrivances.

And then there were The Bird People . . .

The Bird People The Bird People The Bird People.

I hesitate to comment on them. I would be lying if I said there wasn't a lingering fear after seeing—dreaming—(inventing?)—them. The encounter left me with sensorial eruptions battling not one another but the very mechanisms of sensory delivery. These Bird People, with one synchronized glance, relayed an implied *capability* of something both above and below retribution. No, I don't think I'll discuss them further.

I dreamed I was a simulation critic. One with the clout to make or break a simulation: to bless it, co-sign it, and watch it spread across B; or to ignore it, deprive it of oxygen, and watch it asphyxiate.

In this dream I was blindfolded and ferried to yet another dream in order to review a soon-to-be-released simulation named *Ca'bal*. How I knew the name of this simulation—always a well-guarded secret, even to influential critics—was left unexplained by my dream.

I was then, as happens in dreams, further along the timeline.

I was in the simulation.

I was in a trattoria, or maybe a roadhouse. The dining room was half-full and candle-lit. All two-tops. Only instead of dinner tables the diners were separated by marble slabs an artisan short of sarcophagi. Across from each diner was a version of themselves—across from me was a version of myself. Our dream selves. These dreams smiled and laid themselves out on the marble. It was understood that we were supposed to feast, and everyone else did. There were no screams, no pain, only wine and place settings. The intended symbolism, the coded healing and guided journey, won over the others but fell flat with me. I pushed away my cutlery and noticed the frustration on my better's face—and he, I dreamed, noticed the resignation on mine.

Further along, blindfolded again in the ferry, I dreamed I ate myself and dreamed I was healed . . . dreamed that B was no simulation, that B was the genesis of every simulation . . . dreamed I was no longer famished and dreamed I'd withheld oxygen from my review of *Ca'bal*.

SALAI THE SECOND

Salai the Second, son of Salai the Slayer, lives in perpetuity as a quotidian metronome for the citizens of Salai. These citizens, possessing a unique temporal disposition that began long before the beheading of Salai the Second at the behest of his father Salai the Slayer, wake every day with no knowledge of time . . . until they recall that it took exactly one second for Salai the Second's head to fall. From there they expand to minutes and hours and begin their day.

Future generations of Salai will split into two warring factions: one drunk on the conviction that the beheading of Salai the Second by his father, Salai the Slayer, was an act of kindness, a generous bequeathing of order to those otherwise doomed to chaos; the other faction unflinching in their conviction that the beheading of Salai the Second, the dogmatic *capitation* of time, banished all of Salai from a timeless utopia.

MASS ADDICTION: NEWSELF

NewSelf was introduced in a university town as a university experiment conducted in a university manner that yielded university results.

NewSelf was a nanocorpus worn over one's skin that randomly selected other users of NewSelf to shuffle appearances with: Joe became Sue became Betsy became Leonard became Elvira. The psychological benefits and challenges were as expected, and so was—at least for Self, the parent company of NewSelf—the hack and subsequent leak.

Black market NewSelf nanocorpi flooded other university towns then major cities then remote villages and deep-sea colonies. Soon after there was another hack that allowed users of NewSelf to *choose* their new self from the database of all whom had used NewSelf in the past. And soon after that there was another hack that allowed users of NewSelf to choose their new self from the database of all whom had used not only NewSelf but Self . . . and that was ninety-nine percent of B.

The end result of this small university experiment gone planetary was that a majority of those inhabiting B now looked like one of the dozen or so most popular users of Self.

The final hack was no hack at all but was indeed called "the final hack" deep inside the user agreement all users of NewSelf had signed. This non-hack provided a sixteen-hour window for all users of NewSelf to decide if they wanted to go back to their former self or remain—forever—as the new self they had chosen. If they chose to go back to their former self they would have no future access to Self or any of its subsidiaries, including NewSelf. You can imagine how this played out.

BESTIARY: THE SWAILER

Calling to mind the worst parts of a rabid weed, calcified regret, and tropical stroke, the Swailer was a semi-domesticated virus that roamed the streets and frequented the degenerate watering holes of B's most desperate simulations looking for a handout. The Swailer had no redeeming qualities and often smelled of illicit growth. The Swailer did have one quality more brutal than the rest: the Swailer mimicked words, but only the worst of words and only in the register of a deathbed demon wailing its final hail to the Underworld. This wail caused both drop-dead heart attacks and religious conversions. It also sustained the Swailer, as he was often given scraps of insight and specks of lunar dust with the understanding that he'd move on and bring his wail with him.

DECADENCE & LITERATURE & GENOCIDAL SPAS

During B's last cycle of global decadence music went extinct: *slow then slower then all-at-once.* There was no demand for notes, rhythms or sonic storytelling. Music was not missed, not venerated, only referenced as one referenced instincts or amour fou or spatial intelligence.

This presented a great opportunity for a pair of genocidal technologists bound by marriage.

•

Femo was the inventor of Orgapp. (Much like simucide, Orgapp was first illegal then tolerated then legitimized via tax breaks.) Orgapp turned Femo into a proclivarch (it turns out orgasms on demand are highly addictive) and the ultimate dinner guest. Half of B's population was on Orgapp and at least half of those were highly addicted. Orgapp became a political issue, with supporters and detractors often coming to blows: not so much over its orgasmics, but over its collecting of data—over its knowing what, *exactly and neurologically*, got everyone off.

Loma was the inventor of Appapp. Appapp was not the first app to promise unmitigated approval but Appapp was the first to promise approval on an addiction- and depression-free basis:

"All Ups No Downs." This was, from the beginning, the wink of all winks. All users of Appapp knew they'd soon be addicted and no one cared. It's estimated that ninety percent of B was on Appapp and most of them were highly addicted and "depression free" evolved to "depression low" to "depression high" to "suicide probable." Loma became a bona fide proclivarch. Appapp may have led to increased suicide rates but it delivered and delivered and—*exactly and neurologically*—damn well delivered.

The blowback that first hit Orgapp and Femo spread to Appapp and Loma. *Privacy! Suicide!* The couple were lumped together, the married mercenaries: "The FeLoing of society." Of course about half of society saw no problems at all: *Orgasms and Approval on demand? Yes please!* Femo and Loma were under no legal or financial threats, only a threat to their place—and they loved their place. One might even say they were addicted to it.

And so they decided to bring back music. They decided *that* would be their legacy: their great wash, their philanthropic sweat lodge.

The couple poured their money and connections into their own FeLoing of society: FeLo Concerts and FeLo Music Programs and FeLo Scholarships and the FeLo Record Label and the FeLo Awards and FeLo wings of universities. The FeLo logo—with various members of the bestiary wrapped around the F and L— came to represent not only music history and the pursuit of musical excellence, but the very artform itself.

Users of Orgapp continued to have orgasms on demand

and sexual interaction continued to fall and Orgapp breaks and Orgapp rooms became part of any modern business, housing complex, or government building. Users of Appapp continued to live in states of higher and higher approval until the very moment they offed themselves.

The population declined. Legacies were secured.

TAMPEDUSA / ZAMPEDUSA

THE TOWN OF TAMPEDUSA

Tampedusans invented the hundred hour clock which is often referred to as the hundred hour day and is less often referred to as the hundred hour creative spurt—*hundred hour spurt* having been usurped by those claiming to host the hundred hour sex party of the same name in the adjacent town of Zampedusa, although everyone knows Zampedusans are perverts and pathological liars. But all of that is of little interest. What's of big interest is what happens outside those hundred hours: no one in the town, the town of Tampedusa, has any clue. There are traditionalists that believe there is simply sleep, and in a town that has turned circadian rhythm into militant circadian alignment, who cares about time while all are sleeping. And then there are those that believe time itself stands still at the end of the hundred hour clock's revolution and begins again upon the clock's next tick. For those, the question becomes: How long does time stand still? And: What takes place during the time of no time? And, of course: Why?

Zampedusans are neither perverts nor liars but are pathological in their pursuit of all things not Tampedusan. In other words: they are only interested in that which exists outside the hundred hour clock invented by the Tampedusans. In fact, *they* only exist outside the Tampedusan clock. All talk of sex parties and *hundred hour spurts* was devised with the sole purpose of discouraging Tampedusan meddling. (Not that there aren't sex parties, but they are of a more classic variety and humble duration.) Zampedusans are of one mind on this, if for no other reason than there is but one original Zampedusan—Zampedusa—and she has mined the extremities of her nature to engineer a town that lives inside a time that does not exist in Tampedusa.

CREATOR

Woman X and Man Y like to roleplay. They began roleplaying soon after it was discovered that B—all of B—is a virtual construct. X and Y figured: *Might as well enjoy it.*

They began small: hands tied to bedpost, then hands and feet; masks of the bestiary, then full costumes. Things took a more extreme turn when Creator hit the market. Per the user agreement, Creator was designed to "Discover the motivations that drove the creator of our virtual construct." The creators of Creator hoped that by logging all of the virtual worlds created by all the users of Creator they could "work backward" and discover what motivations a higher being might have to create *this*. The only steadfast rule of Creator was that there was one creator per virtual construct, per game: all other players were subject to that creator's vision and only that creator could end that reality, end that game.

X and Y did the superhero thing, the rescued from a brothel thing, the space travelers thing, the aristocracy thing, the new money thing, the assassins for hire thing, things things things. Then X suggested they do the torture fantasy thing, with her as the torturer. Y, always game, hesitated then stalled under cover of "precedents" and "poking Pandora." X persisted and Y acquiesced and admitted that he'd fantasized about torturing X and they both agreed that could come next.

And so X created a world inside Creator where she tortured Y . . .

It was brutal, unmeasured, and creative. Y was left broken and weeping inside a cheap hotel room. The cops came. Statements were given. Y played along, played his role, as he waited for X to end the game. Waited and waited. The cops insisted on a polygraph which Y failed—the story he told them, after all, wasn't true. After days (weeks?) Y finally broke down and told the cops the truth: they were all inside of a virtual construct devised by X where she tortures him, and only X can end the virtual construct.

Y was sent to a madhouse that specializes in treating its patients with a form of therapy called Looped Acceptance (LA) that reenacts the patient's delusion again and again, day after day. Between LA sessions that left Y broken and weeping inside a cheap hotel room, he was forced to participate in group therapy sessions where participants took turns reading aloud then discussing that day's news—forcing them to live inside what the madhouse deemed reality. As it so happened, the front page news each day focused on two narratives: one centered around a conglomerate of leading scientists and philosophers pronouncing that "We *do not* live inside a virtual construct"; the other narrative focused on the exploits of X, the creator of the world's first "unique to user virtual construct game, Creator."

It's unknown if X ever ended the game.

BESTIARY: THE LYRIM

The Lyrim was once a bird of prey. Over time the Lyrim lost its fangs and its claws and its stinger and, eventually, its ability to fly. Once measuring two meters, the domesticated Lyrim topped out at no more than a foot. The Lyrim did, however, acquire the ability to whisper midnight chants of discouragement into its owner's ear. A typical night for a Lyrim began with feigned sleep inside its "floor nest" at the foot of its owner's bed. Once its owner was asleep, the Lyrim hopped onto the bed then waddled over to its owner's ear and whispered something along the lines of: *May your dreams die like flight / Your worth fall like fangs / Your sex have no night / Your shame free to harangue.* Most Lyrim owners lived alone and were beset with mental challenges and either hanged themselves or felt the need to release their pet Lyrim into the wild. Within a few generations the Lyrim regained its fangs and claws and stinger and began to fly and continued to prey.

IRORI

A meteorite shower off the coast of B's smallest land mass produced a phenomenon unrecorded before or since. The impact unleashed—either by force or alchemical reaction—a previously dormant fungal species upon the nearest inhabitants. These fungi bonded to the islanders' nervous system and elicited—*dictated*—a life of rigid and unwavering symmetry: a third of their lives were spent in deep sleep, a third of their lives were spent in a state of peaceful community-building, a third of their lives were spent in a rabid state of masochistic scheming and self-flagellating that ceased only upon another deep sleep.

No two of the fungal-fused islanders were on the same schedule. There was much overlap, some more than others, but invariably a contemplative hair-twirling olive branch spinner would encounter a band of gesticulating teeth-mashers and attempt to reason with the reptilian-minded heathens only to observe them, one by one, pass into a deep sleep after which they woke to the former peacekeeper smashing his face with a meteorite as they returned fire with *Ohm* after palm-raised *Ohm*.

Scientists, politicians, and clergy from B's self-proclaimed "most advanced region," upon hearing of this "natural" / "systemic" / "holy" phenomenon, agreed that it would be to their mutual long-term benefit to assign these islanders to cities and towns and villages of their collective choosing.

MU'TIO'S CODA

The line snaked through fields of processing towers, below a sky of hypnodrones, and towards the village God.

Small talk amongst the queuing citizens of Mu'Tio was not unlike the small talk amongst citizens of Mu'Tio every Post Election Day: pleasant, communal, downright cheery. A typical exchange praised the notion of following democratic norms and endorsed Post Election Day as the day—the real day—that was done.

The village of Mu'Tio was B's first simulation democracy: its simulation was decided by popular vote every sixteen years; unless, of course, the new simulation dictated it was decided every two years or four years or, like the last simulation, every sixteen days. The finalists on this year's ballot were POST-APOCALYPTIC REBUILD and PRE-APOCALYPTIC DECADENCE.

Decadence won by a slim margin and the processing towers and hypnodrones got to work and the citizens of Mu'Tio dutifully waited their turn to kneel in front of the village God and have their reality filters adjusted *just so*: just enough to allow the newly elected simulation to wash over them without drowning them.

•

Contrary to the doctrine espoused by academics that study Mu'Tio, these simulations more often than not brought the citizens of Mu'Tio *closer* to reality, as reality will be defined in much later histories.

LAOOA

Laooa, more a naturalist and illustrator than a scientist, claimed to have solved the riddle of perpetual motion. How she came about this solve she swore to never reveal. What this solve was she promised to the highest bidder—payment upfront. And so Laooa began a worldwide tour of wooing and being wooed: Presidents and Prime Ministers, Kings and Queens, Dictators and Theocrats, Warlords and Theosophists. Though no formal offers were made many offerings were made, and with them Laooa perpetuated her riddle.

REVIEW: TANTONINO

Tantonino is the pen name of the writer that brought both the novel—the transporting kind—and sex—the fucking kind—back to a region of B that had mirrored its lesser self then lost its way under a wave of hysteric pseudo-utilitarian morals.

The novel as artform wasn't banned exactly, it had just been downgraded by unseen consensus and exiled to algorithmic gulags by way of academic perversion. Tantonino's *Tantonino* changed all that. Of course no one had ever seen Tantonino and there was no record of his "real name" and, in the libertine spirit of *Tantonino's* revolution, no one cared.

For the tenth anniversary of the publication of Tantonino's *Tantonino*, festivals were planned, rendezvous were arranged, and moralists of all stripes were burned in effigy and satirized in impromptu feats of burlesque acrobatics.

Only later, much later, was it revealed that there were many versions of *Tantonino*. In fact, there were as many version of Tantonino's *Tantonino* as there were readers. The book, by way of hypnosis and cadenced sorcery, was proven to morph its sexual bits—most of its bits—to fit the desires of its readers.

Philosophers often argue that such trickery disqualifies *Tantonino* from in fact being a novel, but those philosophers are from other regions of B.

CooC

CooC is a circle
that never overlaps
yes yes yes
she bookends in caps

. . . the circle artist CooC transmuted . . . passing from the shared invention of ghouls and poets and serfs and mystics into, well . . . at her coming out party cloaked as a solo exhibition, the self-titled *CooC*, she floated above the crowd, twisting and turning and, depending on one's relationship with light, appearing as a perfect line or a perfect crescent or a perfect hemisphere or a perfect circle . . . to most she appeared not at all, although they would later claim she appeared to them in dreams as . . .

OPERA THEORY

B's most revered text is an opera written by an AI performance artist under the influence of a solar flare that melted her neural network as she let rip with a singular death rattle that compressed all of B's sacred data into an ephemeral and triumphant musical euphoria.

All this is well known, as are the subsequent skirmishes over the meaning, dominion, and cosmological implications of the opera. The opera, however, has never been performed . . . unless one adheres to the theory that the opera *is* B and that B will always be under the influence of AI performance art.

THE DEMON TRIBE

A tribe predating B's first Lava Age cut out newborn tongues, chopped off expressing hands, and gouged out contact-seeking eyes. This tribe was known to the surrounding tribes as The Demon Tribe, not due to its customs regarding tongues, hands, and eyes—The Demon Tribe was, in many ways, *less* severe than its neighbors—but due to its belief that all living creatures on B had an attendant demon. The Demon Tribe's only sacrament, only liturgy, only ceremony, was the quest to seduce, subvert and become its demon. This quest, always undertaken without tongue and often undertaken without hands or eyes, was completed by the few, and only, members of The Demon Tribe, or any tribe, to survive the first Lava Age. Whether or not this trinity of seduction, subversion, and survival truly transformed one into its demon—thus making all living creatures on B the spawn of demons—is best contemplated under extreme states of lunar dust withdrawal, deep inside an expressionless hell where data voids creation.

GO'GAI GAI'GO

Go'Gai Gai'Go was a failed martyr, philandering mystic, latent theosophist and, penultimately, first of the Menti Mani. He hailed from an unnamed swamp region that oscillated between B's western and eastern hemispheres. This oscillation would cause many skirmishes between the Go'Gai tribe and the Gai'Go tribe, but that was on another timeline. (On yet another timeline, one in the distant diagonal, the swamp region was an immobile lakebed of undiscovered lunar dust, but that timeline ends before it intersects with ours.)

Having failed, repeatedly, to drown himself in the agnosticism of muddy waters, Go'Gai Gai'Go set forth on a quest to discover what existed beyond unnamed swamps: he discovered money.

Go'Gai Gai'Go took to money like morality to a timeline. He *understood* money: every illicit nook and tacit cranny. But what he intuited most was money's relationship to sagacity, and so he set about inhabiting The Sage—or at least her guises. This went over quite well and led Go'Gai Gai'Go to the penultimate portion of his quest: founding the Menti Mani.

For an astronomical sum the Menti Mani laid holy hands on true believers, and since true believers of the Menti Mani believed Go'Gai Gai'Go's declaration that space was an illusory construct, the Menti Mani were always close by, ready to lay holy hands.

It turns out that on B, at least on this timeline, anytime Belief reaches a critical mass it usurps any previous agreements on reality. (Whether or not that belief changes reality or masks reality is unknown.) This, ultimately, did not bode well for Go'Gai Gai'Go.

The belief that space did not exist spread like a solar flare, and for a brief period holy hands were laid on true believers. This absence of space turned out to be democratic in nature, and once this was discovered Go'Gai Gai'Go was strangled in his sleep.

LUNAR DUST WITHDRAWAL

On occasion, the various lunar dusts I utilize to access diagonal dimensions are nowhere to be found. The withdrawal that ensues leaves no visible scars but is marked by intense auditory, visual and extrasensory hallucinations of—(from within?)—a dimension hellbent on diminishing returns, a dimension of calculated convictions and discombobulated demands.

This—perhaps *headspace* more than dimension—is, at best, an unfortunate place to spend one's time. At worst, it's a fruitless rootless hootless bardo: a headspace of formulaics dressed as progressions and baselines sauntering as breakthroughs, a headspace of narratives seeking salvation.

There are tales, often whispered in verse, passed amongst fellow travelers along Highway B that speak of a perpetual pigeonhole, a lunar dustless lethargy metastasizing mendacity. Tales of being locked-in to semantic postures and pandering poses and cut off from Highway B. Tales of a hell of bells and whistles administered by peddlers of the cure.

My recent dry period tripping out inside this dissociative realm—one which the locals refer to quite confidently as Reality—was marked by an unholy clusterfuck of shapeshifting gnostics abetted by ravenous technologies seeking neurological footholds. This headspace lacks—*is immune to*—original thought yet loops in maleficent hypnoses of increasing acuity. This headspace vilifies Other yet eulogizes her shadow. This headspace genuflects at the altar of Santo Secular while molding deities in her likeness.

It's best to avoid withdrawal from lunar dust. It's wise to stock up. It's recommended that one elude sanctioned sirens. Post withdrawal, should one locate more lunar dust—should one avoid the perpetual pigeonhole—one must mythologize one's way to sanity.

HORRORFEST

Jingle #1

Every fourth Gregorian
Get your horror in

Beheadings & betrayals, pimps & plagues
No justice my darlings, you're beyond the Hague
Defenestrations galore & castrations ashore
You're crying! You're dying! What a rabid bore!

Transgressive dandies & conniving zingari
Oh schatzi, burn that letter, you know what she means to me!
Too late strega, I've you over the lava
Now repeat after me: Haha! Haha!

Every fourth Gregorian
Get your horror in

The Classics Stage

Temporal dysmorphia disfigures Finn's reality and bathes her neurochemistry in a putrid color that sounds and smells like the reverberating finale unfolding before the Classics Stage at a horrorfest where Finn and The Infinite Finns are scalped and boiled.

"Scoiling" is all Finn hears from the chorus as skulls singe and skin bubbles and The Infinite Finns giggle-gag-wail penultimate communal agony from the respitic bowels of the classic children's sing-along:

Sco' Sco' Scoiling
in the mind of B . . .
Smo' Smo' Smoke your dust
lunar as can be . . .

Back at the Satellite Villa

A medley of conjured sunrises beam throughout the satellite villa
and nourish an adjacent field of obedient Tiger Lilies in full bloom
as B smokes his lunar dust and asks the mirror that float-follows
him around if it's indecent to stage a horrorfest every four days—
if it's unwise to dream infinite Finns inside finite dreams.

The Infinite Finns drag pieces of their oozing selves along: eye sockets, ear remnants, fallen kneecaps: melting, scoiling, gurgle-yelp-singing verses that end in *On to Die* and *Tangent Lie* and other sour-graping death's door Knock Knocks . . .

> *Who's there?*
> *Scoiling death.*
> *Scoiling death who?*
> *Scoiling death upon You!*

Finn holds together the goo that has become her face and the brain that has become her fou and *Cry Cry Cries* her way through the caroling crowd, stumbles up to the edge of the dream, peers through the mirror at B and simmering-jaw pleads *Why oh Why?*

Jingle #2

Every fourth Gregorian
Get your horror in

Deluded by stoic Meteor—or was it Viral eyes?
Diagonal Dimensions?—lies lies lies
We're singing for you Finn, in that sirenverse key of yonic
Come to me cara, tell yourself it's shamanic

Scoiling whys & one-way byes
Oh Finn, you were never versaic—sigh sigh sigh
"Read my letter! It's much better!"
Stai zitta bamba! & perhaps we'll let her!

Every fourth Gregorian
Get your horror in

The All About B Stage

A spotlit smiling tuxedoed shiney-shoed and tophatted B tap-dances atop a stage of concentric dreams.

The Infinite Finns and their ambered agony make up the chorus.

The shadow you see is cast by sadism.

The Finn you see is cast as audience.

B stops tapping, discards the smile and lays out his dreams like a sunbathing deck of lunar dust tarot poolside at an embalming.

The Infinite Finns sing:

Pull a card, sight unseen
Pull a card, it's just a dream
We were Finn, once we were
You'll be us, don't demur

Finn thinks this must be one of those rewire-some-neural-pathways spaces of reanimation: light dark frame shapeless purpose nihilism narcissism narcissism.

The Infinite Finns sing:

Perhaps it is, but just for B
Have some dust, then you'll see
That's the dream, thought you knew
If you don't dream B, he'll dream you

The Infinite Finns appear from the shadows, tapdance

around Finn and repeat: *He'll dream you . . . He'll dream you . . . If you don't dream B, he'll dream you . . .*

Back at the Satellite Villa

B's mirror floats in front of him, Nihilo's North Star: a photonic dictator sculpting horrors.

Smoke Break

. . . He'll dream you . . . He'll dream you . . .

. . . Finn walks the perimeter of the horrorfest, of B's dream, past stage upon stage upon jam-packed horrorfest stage . . . walks in the shoes of The Infinite Finns and their jingled warnings, walks through the shadows and away from the audience caste . . . walks beyond the perimeter of the horrorfest, beyond B's dream . . .

. . . If you don't dream B, he'll dream you . . .

Jingle #3

Every fourth Gregorian
Get your horror in

Drool hangs down . . . drool hangs down
Clowns in town . . . seeking padded sound
Finn it's for you . . . you & you
Koo-Koo-Koo . . . Koo-Koo-Koo

Choirs & knocks & clocks a nil
You're free to go, save the will
B's a'liting & a'lauding
His floating mirror, autoapplauding

Every fourth Gregorian
Get your horror in

Finn smokes her lunar dust and dreams she's an enchantress atop a horrorfest stage with one spell to cast. One spell to save her from the giggle-gag jingling infinite chorus into which *she's* been cast.

She knows she's been here before.

She knows consciousness comes before language, before spells and before spelling.

She knows if she doesn't dream B he'll dream her.

Finn casts her spell: she dreams a B in pursuit of infinite journeys to diagonal dimensions for no other reason than to tell their tales . . . dreams these ephemeralities are B's only purpose . . . dreams she's the narrator and it goes like this . . .

HIGHWAY B CREATION MYTH

An extinction event—some say meteor, others claim attuned misanthropy—ended life on a planet commonly referred to as B. Along with engulfing B's flora and fauna, the flames seen and unseen annihilated the planet's collective narrative: archetypes, mythologies, dialects, religions, persecutions, art, histories true or invented . . . annihilated all byproducts of carbon-based filters.

The consciousness of the planet, it turned out, would not, *could* not, capitulate to a mere extinction event . . . refused to follow its creations, its placeholders and perverted simulacrums. The consciousness of B carried on, ensnared in a grand in-between, cast into myriad diagonal dimensions wrestling for order and influence over what was to be remembered and what was to come next, what would be encoded into memories cellular and frequencial: what was to come of a palimpsested planet.

This planetary consciousness—chaotic and concussed—was nothing like it had been "in the beginning" because there was no beginning: *time* never existed beyond its function as an agreed upon currency.

Finn's lucidity lulls and her dream is breached by an approaching chorus singing of *Four wise moons / Miraging blooms / Lunar dust swoons / Vagabond goons* and Finn knows her doppleganging infinite doesn't adhere to creation myths, timeless or otherwise.

This consciousness needed to regain its fighting form after delegating its ferocity to melancholic underlings . . . needed to regain its reckless and raconteuring nature . . . the planet needed a focal point for narrative autonomy . . .

Finn dreams that all tales are origin tales and all myths are creation myths and she dreams this out of self-preservation.

> . . . a narrator unable to linger . . . a narrator exploring
> diagonal dimensions along Highway B at the behest of a
> collective dream's resurrection . . .

Finn's dream pauses, or runs its course. The chorus is here with all of their *If you don't dream B, he'll dream yous* and she isn't sure if she's dreaming B or he's dreaming her. Finn isn't sure why she's here but if it's true that time doesn't exist it exists even less if one runs out of it.

Back at the Satellite Villa

B's mirror hums the notes to a horrorfest and leads the chorus in a ghoulish rendition of Highway B Blues.

The dreams of Finn and B collapse into psychosomatic jingles.

Jingle #4

Every fourth Gregorian
Get your horror in

Dream me dreamy miny Finn
Choose a mirror by its grin
Choose dimensions by their sin
Dreamer dreamer where is Finn?

Dreamer dreamer what of B?
Performing a' long Highway B
Finns & mirrors, Maestro B
Living right inside of thee

Every fourth Gregorian
Get your horror in

Finn is back at the satellite villa reflecting a medley of conjured sunsets adjacent a field of Tiger Lilies in spring's final bloom.

Back at the Satellite Villa

B smokes his lunar dust and allows Chaos her space and instructs Order to reset the metronome to HORRORFEST:

Horrorfest

The Infinite Finns sing:

> *Every fourth Gregorian*
> *Get your horror in*
>
> *Rapacious tales & metronomes*
> *Highway B's mass o' gnomes*
> *'Chistic wiffs of cryptic tomes*
> *Say "distich talk & cazzo cloans"*

The Infinite Finns scream:

> *Scoiled bones & soiled loans!*
> *Gallows casting holo ohms!*
> *Plebeians & Persephones!*
> *Aesthetes staging cazzo cloans!*
>
> *Every fourth Gregorian*
> *Get your horror in*

MORE FROM ARCHWAY EDITIONS

Ishmael Reed – *The Haunting of Lin-Manuel Miranda*
Unpublishable (edited by Chris Molnar and Etan Nechin)
Gabriel Kruis – *Acid Virga*
Erin Taylor – *Bimboland*
NDA: An Autofiction Anthology (edited by Caitlin Forst)
Mike Sacks – *Randy*
Mike Sacks – *Stinker Lets Loose*
Paul Schrader – *First Reformed*
Archways 1 (edited by Chris Molnar and Nicodemus Nicoludis)
Stacy Szymaszek – *Famous Hermits*
cokemachineglow (edited by Clayton Purdom)
Ishmael Reed – *Life Among the Aryans*
Alice Notley – *Runes and Chords*

Archway Editions can be found at your local bookstore or ordered directly through Simon & Schuster.

Questions? Comments? Concerns? Send correspondence to:

> Archway Editions
> c/o powerHouse Books
> 220 36th St., Building #2
> Brooklyn, NY
> 11232